The Pig in a Wig

ned on or before

Alan MacDonald

Illustrated by Paul Hess

MACDONALD YOUNG BOOKS

Once some animals lived on a farm in a humble, tumbledown barn. One of them was a pig called Peggoty. Peggoty was a kind-hearted pig, but she was rather proud of her looks and she would spend hours admiring her reflection in the duck pond. She secretly believed herself to be the prettiest, pinkest, most perfect pig in all the world.

One spring morning some young lambs passed
the farmyard gate on their way to the fields.
Peggoty was gazing at herself in the duck pond
as usual. The lambs stopped to stare at her.
They were very pleased with their new woolly
coats and hadn't yet learned any manners.
'Look at the fat ol' pig,' said one.
    'Look at her big snorty snout.'
    'Isn't she ugly?' they said.
    Peggoty didn't hear them,
until one lamb started to bleat
a song and the others joined in.

'Ugly ol' pig, bet you smell,
You're pink and
fat and you're
bald as well!!'

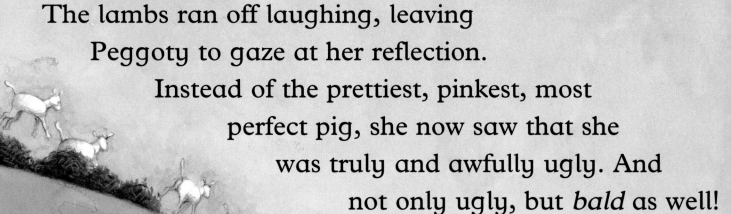

The lambs ran off laughing, leaving
Peggoty to gaze at her reflection.
Instead of the prettiest, pinkest, most
perfect pig, she now saw that she
was truly and awfully ugly. And
not only ugly, but *bald* as well!

A tear trickled down her snout
and plopped into the duckpond.
Why had she been born bald? There
must have been some mistake. She dried
her eyes and decided to ask the wise old horse
who knew about such things.

She found the wise old horse munching hay in the barn.

'Excuse me,' said Peggoty, most politely, 'but could you tell me why I am bald?'

'Bald? Ah yes,' said the wise old
horse, who spoke horribly slow.
　'The reason you're bald is
perfectly plain,
　They must have forgotten to
give you a mane.'
　'And please, is that what
makes me so awfully ugly?'
asked Peggoty.
　'Why of course,' said the horse,
'there is no finer thing in all the
world than a glossy and
galloping mane.'
　Peggoty trotted into the yard
where she met . . .

. . . the marmalade cat, curled up in the shade.

'Excuse me,' said Peggoty, most politely, 'but do you know why I am bald?'

The marmalade cat opened one eye and looked at Peggoty.

'The reason you're bald is right under your nose,
    You're wearing no fur from your tail to your toes.'

Peggoty nodded sadly. 'And is that what makes me so awfully ugly?'

'Of course,' purred the cat, 'there is no finer thing in the world than lickable, tickable fur.'

For the rest of that day Peggoty hid herself from the other animals. It was after dark when she returned to the humble, tumbledown barn. Only the moon was out.

'Oh luminous moon,' sighed Peggoty, 'why was I born so bald and awfully ugly?'

To her great surprise a voice sang back,
'The reason is perfectly simple to sing,
You have no feathers on either wing.'
Peggoty looked up. It wasn't the moon talking after all, it was the singing cock on the roof.

'Can you help me?'
asked Peggoty. 'I've
asked everyone why
I'm bald and awfully
ugly and they say it's
because I haven't got
a glossy and galloping
mane or lickable
tickable fur, not to
mention feathers on
either wing. But I
don't see what I can
do about it.'

The cock strutted up
and down on the roof.
It sang:

'It would indeed be a strange
and wonderful sight,
If a pig could grow feathers
overnight.'

Suddenly Peggoty's tail began
to twitch the way it did when she
had an idea. Without bidding the
singing cock goodnight, she ran
into the barn.

All that night, while the other
animals slept, strange rustling and
scuffling sounds came from
Peggoty's corner.

When the first sunlight crept into
the barn, the cock crowed and the
animals came out into the yard.
Everyone stared at Peggoty.
Overnight she had grown hair.
Golden locks of hair as curly
as a pig's tail. Peggoty tossed
her head proudly and paraded
in front of them.

Just then the young lambs passed by the gate, following their mother up to the fields.

'Look at the pig!' shouted one.

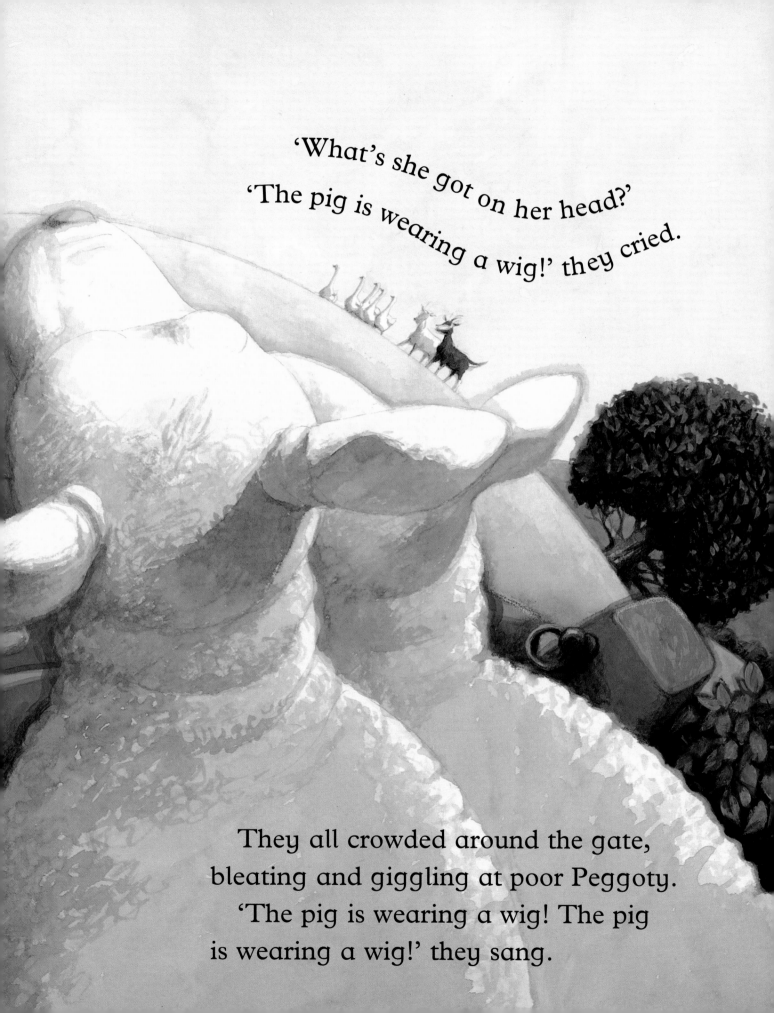

'What's she got on her head?'
'The pig is wearing a wig!' they cried.

They all crowded around the gate,
bleating and giggling at poor Peggoty.
'The pig is wearing a wig! The pig
is wearing a wig!' they sang.

Peggoty's pink face turned red.
She took to her trotters and fled up
the hill. She didn't stop running
until she reached the big
farmhouse at the top. There she
crept into the shadow of the wall
and wept. Tears ran down her
plump cheeks and the straw wig
sat crooked and crumpled
on her head.

'Waah haah!' a voice wailed nearby.
Peggoty sniffed and listened. Someone
else was crying too. It was coming from
the farmhouse.

'Hush, hush, my poppsie!
Don't cry, my precious,'
she sang.

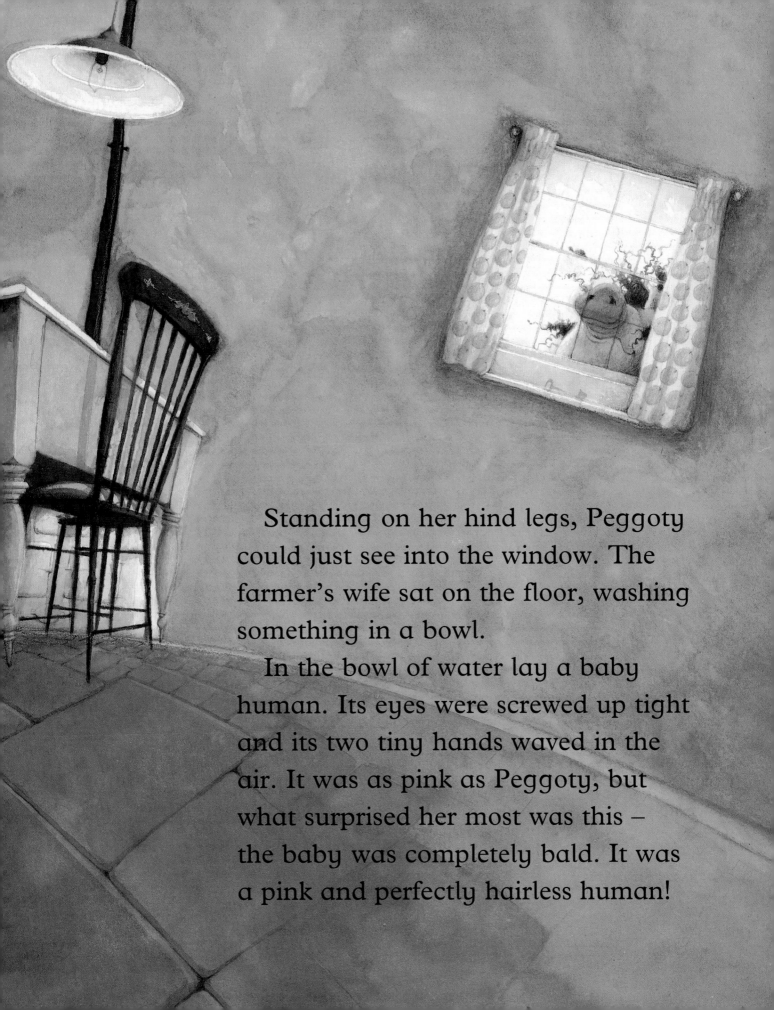

Standing on her hind legs, Peggoty
could just see into the window. The
farmer's wife sat on the floor, washing
something in a bowl.

In the bowl of water lay a baby
human. Its eyes were screwed up tight
and its two tiny hands waved in the
air. It was as pink as Peggoty, but
what surprised her most was this –
the baby was completely bald. It was
a pink and perfectly hairless human!

The farmer's wife tickled the baby's round tummy.
'You're bootiful. My bootiful angel,' she cooed.
The baby began to gurgle and giggle. Peggoty
pressed her face against the glass, smiling back.
At that moment the farmer's wife looked up
and saw the bedraggled, bewigged face at
her window.

'HELP!' she screamed. 'A horrible hairy monster!'

Peggoty fell over backwards with fright. The crooked and crumpled wig fell off. She left it in the mud and ran out through the gate and back down the hill.

That night she told her story to
the other animals in the humble,
tumbledown barn.

   'And so,' she concluded, 'if you
are hairy, humans think you are
a horrible hairy monster, but
if you are bald (and here she
blushed modestly) they call you
a bootiful angel.'

Peggoty has never worn a wig since that day. And she doesn't believe that the finest thing in all the world is a glossy and galloping mane, lickable tickable fur, or feathers on either wing. She thinks that pigs are born just perfect.

First published in Great Britain in 1998 by
Macdonald Young Books
an imprint of Wayland Publishers Ltd
61 Western Road
Hove
East Sussex
BN3 1JD

Find Macdonald Young Books on the Internet at http://www.myb.co.uk

Printed and bound in Belgium by Proost International Book Co.
British Library Cataloguing in Publication Data available.

ISBN: 0 7500 2452 6